Micro-Waves II

By

John F King

Micro-Waves II

A collection of micro fiction

©*John F King*

York Europe Publishing

2022

ISBN

978-1-8383426-2-3

www.johnkinginternational.co.uk

Contents

'..All this burden of past experience one trails about with one, there ought to be some way of getting rid of one's superfluous memories..'

Aldous Huxley

Eyeless in Gaza

'..Once you accept that you have chosen to be as you are, incredible as that seems, then regret is not possible.'

Arthur Miller

Plain Girl

Micro-Waves II

Back Up

'Caution vehicle reversing' the voice, repetitive, robotic. As the removal van backed into the drive I felt this is an end beginning.

When you left all that remained was possessions. Usual, books, vinyl I should have decimated long ago before the space was empty.

As the vehicle came to a halt I thought of those film scenes when a priest asks a couple if there is any impediment to the marriage and someone actually says something. The past stops the future.

The driver looked first at the boxes then at me, then back to the boxes. Things, no words. You will have to go through with it now. I can see removal people are like doctors or other interstitials – they work on an amalgam of what you tell them and what they see.

My definition of decimation was literal, my estimation. The driver, who had introduced himself as Mervyn and his partner Tariq - ' Life is Moving' it said on the side of their van – looked at the boxes again, then at Tariq. I almost apologised.

After sugar and tea things moved quickly. I admired their system of loading. The Bösendorfer and the Conran were stacked in the storage compartment. It was time for the personal stuff.

'Let me secure that', said Mervyn. Before he sealed the last box he sighted a stranded LP. *Appassionata* sonata, the Barenboim, ' I always preferred the Brendel myself' he said, 'nothing personal.'

I hadn't been as ruthless as I believed, the van which at first sight seemed cavernous was full. Tariq looked at the last container, then me.

He said ' see you in another life.' When we shook hands he planted a small box in my palm.

I'd chosen Antibes because of the story I had read of how Graham Greene would go to the Café Felix there every lunchtime after he has written 500 words.

Plus it was less freighted than Nice, where we had strolled on the prom still listening to each other above the waves of landing jets.

When I saw their van again outside my new studio they were like old friends. They looked at the studio. We could more easily move into the van.

The boxes that couldn't fit in they stacked on the balcony. 'It won't rain tonight' said Mervyn. I don't know where he found the certainty.

The van reversed out of the service road, the robotic voice still advising caution.

The first night I worked the boxes. When I found the *Appassionata* it was the Brendel. I opened the box from Tariq, a continental electrical adaptor.

By the time I reached Chez Felix I had no words just the aperitif.

Black and Red

It was a different kind of snow.

The two canisters descended out of the whiteness.

'Karl-Erik, yours is on the left,' indicated Inge.

Inge opened 'hers' first - explosives, Sten guns.

I released mine - ink, printing plates.

'Words,' said Inge, a tone I couldn't decipher.

The first action of the Occupying Force was to smash up our press.

It felt good to be rolling again.

I delivered at night, leaflets, newspapers at factories, civic buildings flying the wrong flag.

Inge reappeared first light:

'This night come with us. Sub-station, viaduct. Set them back seriously.'

'Reprisals?'

I showed Inge a counter leaflet:

"Terrorists, resisters are traitors. We will find you. Any action against the Force will have fatal consequences."

'Words,' Inge said,

'One day the war will be over. You'll look back and think all you did was write.'

'One day you can think what you want, farewell, Inge.'

I never saw Inge again during the Occupation.

The following Spring I stood next to her in the
ceremonial room of the palace.

The King had aged in exile. He listened intently to the
equerry's briefing before the Prize presentations:

'Sir, award for Karl-Erik, freedom fighter'

'Sir, award for Inge, freedom fighter.'

'Our grateful nation bestows this honour upon you.'

On the fourth Aquavit I said to Inge 'there was a
question that stayed with me throughout the struggle.'

Inge downed the spirit. 'Regret is not in the lexicon.'

'Two canisters fell that first night, how did you know
which was 'mine'?'

Inge's smile returned: ' words fall so beautifully.'

Breaking News

'…back to London. Jane.'

'Berlin, thank you. What times with the press corps in the Hotel Adlon, those Mitte nights, but this show goes out before 9pm UK time…'

'Read the Autocue, Jane. News not show.'

Jane Sleet histrionically touched her In-ear Monitor.

'…Washington, thank you. Still vivid, the blossoms on the Potomac…'

The control room ran the US package. The producer timed her off-air intervention perfectly: 'Read the autocue, Jane or…'

'What? Imagine the show without me.'

The producer indicated three fingers, two, on air…

Jane auto-read live:

'Tonight, immediate, newsreader Jane Sleet to leave TV news.'

'And we are out. Goodnight, Jane.'

Check Off

Talking for a living is hard.

At the close of a day of 1:1 training there are no words.

I am supposed to recognize low and high points in energy levels, why didn't I learn to do it for myself?

It was the lowest cycle in the week, the day, the hour but I thought I could make it before everything closed down.

The check-out worker had a name badge on but I was too scanned out. T , Trevor, Terry…?

'How is your day, are you looking forward to the weekend, anything nice planned?'

I stared back at him in silence. I'm tired, you are too no doubt, who is the training manual spiel for?

I packed my stuff in my *Planet Organic* bag and sloped on. I never looked back. The words 'enjoy your weekend' fell into the aisle.

I practised my apology all night. 'I'm most terribly sorry. Low time. Rude of me.' I could expand this to 'I'm not really like that, you know what customer facing roles are like, how was your weekend, T?' Did he even have one?

Monday same time. It was difficult to contrive to stay in that check-out line.

I only bought one item and the store manager was agitated I wasn't in the four items or fewer lane. When I made it to Trev he said

' how is your day, sir, are you looking forward to the week, anything nice planned?'

I said ' I am most terribly sorry.'

I didn't plan my retirement at the time it happened. I'm at the store at a different time of day now. All the check-outs are automated. I don't know what happened to Trev.

Domed Earth

As catastrophes go it wasn't that bad.

Yet.

Was I the only one on the peninsula who knew there was a countdown? Year, decade, tops.

In stinging air, on cracked earth people laughed at me - 'Kill Joy'.

Almost all visitors arrived by road, petrol, diesel, the hybrids and electrics an afterthought.

Nowhere to go back to. Derelict buildings were brought up. Camper vans became static.

This paradox paradise. Those attracted by the beauty killed it.

The authority's response? Raise the outbound motorway, make 6 lanes in.

Some liked it hot, a mono-season, black Christmas on the beach, the perma-attire of flip-flops. Manufacturers of woollen goods failed, suppliers migrated to the new industries of desalination and aircon, wind turbines as fans.

When the sea decided we were an island it was beyond time for action.

We cycled to the gates of the complex expecting to be resisted by security.

A lonely guard, his asthmatic face illuminated by a screen put down his tablet.

'Join us,' I said.

He offered me two electronic keys, one for each Dome:

'Tropical or Mediterranean?'

The biodomes of the leisure zone had completed their inversion. 'Exotic' plants that flourished inside them were outside, inside were oaks and firs.

I felt so at home in the first Dome I wanted to rename it. Beneath the oak in my old wool coat calling a meeting:

'Agenda, first item, updating our Dome designation.'

The old guard rose: 'first item, electing our leader.'

Gone for It

'Life is too short,' V said.

There was something - K couldn't put his finger on it - that irritated him about this style of speaking but to be irritated is to be fascinated. Afraid too, her way of speaking would rub off on him, he would become the kind of man who said he couldn't put his finger on it.

When V set off for the TV studio that morning K checked in with his own emotions.

'Knock 'em dead, hit 'em for six,' K said but did that mean he wanted her to succeed or fail?

V hadn't returned his goodbye kiss, pulling out from the clinch, the expression 'you only come this way once' already on her lips.

Only weeks before Veronica had been unemployed, redundant. She'd found a new life as a life coach. Her web site hopespringseternal.com a surprise hit launching her from job centre to TV studio in record time.

The studio light showed green – 'you never have a second chance to make a first impression, the journey of a thousand miles begins with a single step' smiled V as she took her place on the sofa.

'You ready for this?' said the presenter, ' quite a journey you've been on.'

'Life isn't a rehearsal,' V shot back.

K put his finger on the remote.

National
Flash
Fiction
Day
18 June 2022

Smirk

It was always there. Never went away to neutral or progressed into open laughter. Just a smirk. It was there when she when up for the prize.

'And now at our biannual political award ceremony the award for…'
The TV screen split into four, showing simultaneous close ups of all 4 nominees.
An anxious face, an eager face, a surprised face and...a smirk. The screen held all 4 in the frames to see who could show how to lose magnanimously best. Of course Rishi knew it wouldn't be her. He felt slightly annoyed for some reason. How awful it would be to want your partner actually to be the runner up.

' …most promising newcomer, from MPs elected at the last general election.'
The presenter feigned difficulty ripping open the envelope.

' Davira Hetherington-Turner. Dav.'
Everyone called her Dav. She simply never answered to any other name, didn't even turn round. Even her partner, Rishi, still thought it was a peculiar name. How could anyone come by it? How could it be invented? Did the vicar mess up the lines at the Christening? Was it designed by her parents to give her a head start in standing out?
Suppose if she'd been a man it would be Dave. Sort of name rarely fully given: Dave, David, Tim, Timothy…

Rishi pulled his thoughts back. She reached the rostrum now. The presenter was acting like a rap MC, asking for more applause as soon as the first wave rippled out. ' Let's hear it. Give it up for Dav.'

Truth was Dav wasn't popular. Not unpopular, not disliked, not likeable.
Some people always get their names shortened, some always get an epithet stuck in front. Hardy, plucky, reliable, thorough. Dav got pushy. Pushy fresher, youngest president of the student union, pushed her way to treasurer of the Labour Club. Attracted all the best speakers from British and European Union -then- politics to the University. Dav always introduced them personally. Next day the press coverage was invariable. Dav on the right of the photograph, plus Cabinet Minister, commissioner, chef de cabinet on the left. Just Dav, the big shot and the smirk.

     At the rostrum Dav tapped the microphone. Rishi hated the way people did that. So histrionic, superfluous, a cliché of a reflex like clearing an unphlemged throat. He knew it was just a trick of the trade. That way people were primed to listen to your first word. Without the tap you could be on your fourth word before people listened to the content. Dav tapped, looked up, then around with that same smirk.

     ' Thanks. Great honour to receive this prize, especially from you hard-faced b'stards,' she said affably,
her arm sweeping across the room full of political journalists who'd elected her to the prize in the first place. ' Everyone should win the best newcomer prize - once.'
She got the laugh she wanted, held the statuette aloft, Oscar -like, for just the right amount of time. Flash cameras went off. She knew what she would look like in the papers the next day. Always did, and always that same bloody …

     'Maybe this will take that smirk off your face,' said the Chancellor the next day with a smile, offering her the most junior of junior ministerial positions in the Treasury.

' Still, greasy pole and all that. Local
Government Finance Bill. First Reading. Then get
it through both houses and the PM and I will see
you right.'
The Bill had graveyard written all over it. Dav,
to whom doubt seemed alien, had it on the statute
books before you knew it. Pushover.
A few well-placed telephone calls, networky
dinners, the right fetes in the right
constituencies. Plus nowadays the alumni lists of
the redbricks could almost match the Oxbridge
boys. First Secretaries didn't exactly succumb to
the charm - Dav knew her limits - but that
expression, that - there is no other word for it
- smirk - you couldn't say no.

     ' The PM will see you now,' said the Number
10 usher. She knew it was a line she would hear
one day
     but even Dav wasn't pushy enough to believe
it would happen so quickly. As she entered the
room the PM and the Chancellor had their backs
turned to her, their gaze fixed outwards across
the Number 10 lawn. Only the Chancellor turned
and spoke.
     ' We knew you could do it, Dav. Nice to have
that bill on the books. Always did hate local
government. Two words that should never be
mixed. Local and government.'
Dav smirked as the Chancellor over- explained his
joke.
The PM spoke for the first time, still not
turning, as if Dav was losing in an attention
competition with the lawn.
     ' Fancy a shot at Cabinet level, Dav?'
The door Dav had been leaning against since being
a fresher opened so simply.

Next day Rishi opened the broadsheets. The photos
showed the PM on the left shaking hands with Dav
on the right.

Same old pose only this time Dav was with a Prime Minister. Took it in her stride though. In the articles below the photos Rishi again noted those timeworn political expressions- graveyard, poisoned chalice, but he always knew Dav would come through.

In the lead up to the next general election Dav focused mainly on the Overseas Aid (Ukraine Reconstruction) Allocation Bill; the Bill which had seen off the two previous ministers. The government was returned with a slightly increased majority. Dav's face had been a feature of many a screen ad and poster. The week after the election she was still in situ in her office high above St James' Park. The stack of red boxes by and on her desk always at exactly the same height, as she worked through and despatched boxes at the same rate as they came in.

Dav had been a Cabinet Minister for nearly a year now as the evening of the political awards came around again. Late that afternoon the Ministerial limo took her directly to her Pimlico flat, picked up Rishi and onto the TV studios. On the way, as Rishi fixed his best cufflinks he wondered why Dav still bothered with prizes. But she never could refuse invites and the convention was an invite meant a prize. After completing the cufflink operation Rishi was able to give her his full attention. Dav was gazing out of the window, her face just so, the expression that hadn't changed all the time he'd known her. He saw his own face in the rear view mirror. The laughter lines, the Campari at lunchtime lines, then back at her. Smirk lines? Who'd ever heard of them? Of course he didn't want her to lose. After all he had climbed the ladder with her. He enjoyed going up, the accompaniments of such a rise easily outnumbered any downside.

So what would the prize be this time? ' Political personality of the year',
' Best cabinet newcomer', ' Most likely PM the election after next…'

Dav swept into the room, a Cabinet Minister now, followed by Rishi and a Principal Private Secretary.
Pleasantries were exchanged, contacts restocked. Awards came up, mostly well deserved and graciously accepted, thank you speeches always that right length and tone, two -liners, the self-deprecation of the confident. All the categories except one had been given out when Rishi next looked across at Dav's still unrewarded face. It was shocking to see her. The smirk vanished, the jaw set, the eyes hard and watery at the same time. The presenter dwelt on the autocue. Then the room as one person saw it coming, transfixed by the unwanted inevitably. The envelope was ripped open and the presenter read out the full name embossed on the card inside.
    'The prize for most promising newcomer goes to Davira Hetherington-Turner.'

Smirk

www.johnkinginternational.co.uk

Micro- Waves II

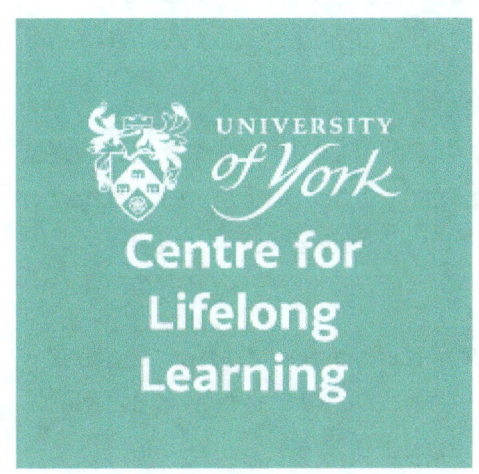

Song Cycle

Centre stage darkness illuminated by approach of off-stage car headlights showing

CONSTANCE

a derelict but retains a hint of a life before, asleep by the overflowing clothes bin in a recycling centre adjacent supermarket. Swish of electric car, brakes, stops. Click of boot and side door opening, **ELLEN***'s shoes on gravel.*

ELLEN *voice off* Clothes like this. The past, the time before, no one needs them now.

ELLEN off, throws bag at the clothes bin. ELLEN doesn't wait to see where bag lands. As doors closing **ELLEN** *'Drive on' to chauffeur, off. Car and lights move away. Bag into view.*

CONSTANCE awakened by voice and bag landing next to her observes but doesn't think it worth moving. It is dawn, centre stage light gradually up. CONSTANCE settles again as car fades to silent.

She is awakened by a theme mobile telephone ring tone. At first CONSTANCE is disorientated and cannot locate the sound but it is coming from the suit bag.

ELLEN *voice as Ansa phone message clicks in*

Ellen Gold, International Artists Management, contact via Zoom. Leave a message if you can't.

Beep. Off.

Phone rings again, same message. CONSTANCE isn't going to get any more sleep. Stirs herself, rummages, ascertains there must be a phone among the clothes bags. Message again. Listens to message. Intrigued. She locates the sound as from the suit bag.

Notes and begins to unzip branded bag. Stops and turns to face out. Light continually rising. It eventually becomes a spotlight.

CONSTANCE

How dare you judge me? You think it couldn't happen to you, think again. I was someone once. Someone real, someone who existed, an artiste. Yes. I was, am. Appearances. That's the past. The time before. Time before it stopped. If your life curved up again when the graph went down I'm pleased for you. Really.

Excuse me.

She turns back to the suit bag. Unzips it and examines it. Begins to extract the clothes within. Lays clothes out. It is a formal suit for classical concerts. She begins to get dressed as for a performance, tentatively then with more confidence as she dresses hums [' Vissi d'arte..']

CONSTANCE *speaking as she puts on the clothes directly over her rags.*

You think it couldn't happen to you, think again. Didn't the crisis bring what was going to happen anyway. It only happened for me sooner. Maybe I had further to fall than you did?

She locates the phone in the inside pocket of the jacket. Message. Presses a button. It plays the music as she is on hold

ELLEN *recorded Ansa phone message* You are in a queue. Your time will come.

CONSTANCE Zoom, what's that? I always did things face to face. That's how I started. That's what finished me. The concert halls were emptying before they became empty. People had been at home too long. They forgot to come out again.

ELLEN *phone message* You are in a queue, your time will come.

CONSTANCE *is now almost fully dressed. Reads out the business card from top of jacket pocket 'EGI Artist Management.' Fully dressed her old form is emerging.*

This must have been meant to happen. There must be a reason.

There has to be. It isn't over until…

The hold theme music stops. There is a beep. CONSTANCE is on. She takes a drink from a bottle and begins to sing into phone as microphone

Beep / Fade

ISBN 978-1-8383426-2-3

York Europe Publishing

 Micro Waves II

2022

J F King

The Captain's Constitutional

Micro-Waves II

www.johnkinginternational.co.uk

York Europe Publishing / The Captain's Constitutional

Staging / FX

Simple staging, lights follow Capt. Salter, FX / Music / street
cries /traffic   tape

Cast

Captain Edward Salter MC

Narrator (of stage directions) and other cast members to be
played / voice by two / three others –

Chatsworth

Telegram boy

Promenaders..

Veteran

Alderman Braithwaite

Sybil

The Captain's Constitutional

Act 1 Scene 1 - INT

Early evening at the Clarence Hotel, Scarborough, Spring 1918

Chatsworth, *the hotel manager reading the Yorkshire Post.*

A calm atmosphere interrupted.

Post Office Telegram boy *enters foyer breathless from cycling*

Boy

Telegram, Telegram, immediate, Captain Edward Salter MC

Chatsworth

Is that noise really necessary, son? Leave that with me. I'll see the Captain receives it immediate.

Boy

War Office it says here, Big Push, recall, I shouldn't wonder

Chatsworth

I'll give you big push if you don't hop it sharpish

Salter *enters from grand staircase, faintly singing 'we're here because we're here because…' full officer's dress, MC ribbon, adjusting cufflinks, dashing. Stops abruptly on seeing telegram boy.*

Salter

Something on, Chatsworth? I've had more peaceful evenings on the Vimy Ridge.

   To boy

Good evening, young man, which outfit you with? King's Own Yorkshire?

Boy

Saluting. I wish. Royal Mail sir, 16 next year, can't wait…

Salter

No doubt the show will be over by then, sunshine. And don't salute me. Not wearing my cap. Regulations. Nothing for me then, Chatsworth?

Chatsworth

Not as yet, sir. Enjoy your constitutional. Fine evening for it, if I may be so bold.

Salter

Thank you Chatsworth. As I said the moment you hear anything…

Chatsworth

Right you are, sir.

Salter saunters out whistling ' Let the great big world keep turning.'

The boy is waiting.

Chatsworth

 He will have the telegram immediately after his evening stroll. Another hour won't change the world. Captain deserves it after all he's been through. Promise, lad.

He offers him a coin.

Scene 2 - EXT

Boy *leaves ringing his bell cheerily as he passes* **Salter** *on the promenade calling out* - Good luck, sir

Salter *on the promenade. Sound of waves, horses, a pleasant evening throng…*

News vendor

Extra, evening special, push for imminent victory?

To Salter. Newspaper sir?

Salter

Not this evening, thank you. I believe I read that one earlier.

News vendor pauses before resuming his cry. Salter strolls on. Humming to himself 'Down at the Old Bull and Bush.' He takes deep breaths of sea air, cordial greetings to everyone he meets:

Local man

Hit 'em for young 'un, you tell 'em from me.

Salter

Good evening my good fellow. And who shall I say told them?

Local girls

1 Hello handsome, buy a girl a drink.

2 Or two

Salter

 Good evening Ladies, I'm sure the quartermaster can muster a dry sherry at my quarters after taking this sea air.

Local girls

giggle, moving on but in earshot La-dee da

The stroll continues convivially, waves, seagulls, brass band playing a music hall melody, he sings along, an automobile backfires, he is momentarily disorientated , manages to resume his singing quietly with difficulty, then sounds recede. He sits quietly on bench facing sea.

Salter reads out the inscription on the bench. 'In Memoriam: to those souls who rested here and found peace in this place.'

Veteran

interrupts his reveries

I am so sorry to disturb your peace sir, do you mind if I join you, not so steady on my pins as I once was. Or should I say pin?

Veteran props his crutches and struggles to salute before sitting.

Salter

No need to salute here soldier, the sea doesn't recognise rank.

Veteran

Nicely put, sir.

They sit contemplating the sound of the waves.

Salter

Where were you, corporal? Forgive me. I shouldn't ask.

Veteran

Kind of you to ask sir. Some new-fangled machine, a tank they call 'em, unexploded shell changed its mind, you can see the result. Or the absence of it.

You sir, I'd be honoured to hear your story? Military Cross!

Salter

That? Oh, nothing.

The sound of the sea

Salter

I would like you to accept a cigarette, young man. Finest tobacco. I had them sent up from London.

He pats his military jacket.

Sorry. I must have left my case in the dugout, digs I mean.

Veteran

Not to worry sir. May I look forward to a smoke with you on your next leave?

Salter

Deo volente. It's my lucky case. Stopped a round in Ypres that had my name on it.

He is becoming agitated.

Must return to my hotel. It has to be there. Lucky you see. Luck.

He is leaving

I have to go, corporal. Forgive me.

He is hurrying along the front, the noises of the promenade seem less convivial, motor vehicles, a military lorry, a dog, the brass band playing a military march… He bumps into a man.

Salter

Excuse me. My error.

Alderman

I say, that you, Captain Salter? Alderman Braithwaite. It was my privilege to present to you the Freedom of Scarborough. I am so pleased to see you exercising it.

Sybil my dear, this is Captain Salter I was telling you of, youngest MC in the British Army. Allow me to present my daughter Sybil.

Salter

Alderman Braithwaite. Miss Sybil, how absolutely enchanting.

Please excuse me.

Alderman

You are in a hurry young man. Anyone would think you were expecting a telegram from the King. A splendid evening for a port at the Grand. Speak up, Sybil.

Sybil

Do join us, Captain, do…

Salter

Please accept my apologies.

From across the road the call of a flower seller

Flower seller

Lavender, lovely lavender, flowers for your sweetheart

Sybil

There be another time, Captain, I'm sure.

Salter

Edward please. I am sorry, where are my manners? What is your favourite flower, Miss Sybil? Something to remember me by.

Alderman

I say, Salter, no call to upset the girl.

Flower Seller

Lovely flowers, flowers for your sweetheart.

Salter

Do you like lavender, Sybil? It is some time since I saw lavender. Wait here a moment. I will be back directly.

Chorus (all the cast members)

Look out, Captain Salter, be careful, comeback, look out

He rushes across the road. Cacophony of noise, heavy motor vehicles, shouts of men.

White noise> The sound of the waves. Fade

The Captain's Constitutional

/Micro-Waves II

The Picture of Dieter Geheimnis

The prison was harder to get into than out of.

Curious considering the crime. No requirement to put alleged in that sentence. People knew the fact, especially him.

The prison door opened from the inside. Dieter Geheimnis sprang out, a determined walk for a man of his age. He crossed the linden-lined street.

I was the first free person he spoke to-

'Direct me… tram stop line 50?'

I waited for him to complete his sentence.

'Please. Excuse me. I've been out of polite society for some time.'

'Evidently' I said, ' No trams here anymore.'

'No trams,' he looked incredulous. I stopped myself feeling sorry for him. There was a silence. I filled it.

'Metro. Things change. Same line.'

'Things change, things stay the same. Are you going this way?'

'No. I have been waiting here for some time.'

'Waiting? But are the vehicles not frequent?'

His face had a blankness about it. Years inside had physically unaltered him. Mentally I couldn't know. I found I neither liked or disliked him.

The silence returned. It wasn't good or bad.

He looked at his watch. Antique not flash, valuable, a family heirloom?

'Are you in a hurry? ' I said. He held my gaze. There was no glint of recognition, then said

'I'm running late. 30 years late…'

He looked at me as if I would understand his reference. He was still speaking as the arrival of the metro overrode his words.

It was 30 years ago today.

Then he looked at me across the crowded courtroom, directly from the dock into the press gallery. The courtroom had been specially built for him and his gang. They seemed to find it droll that tax payers were still paying after what they had inflicted. They all used the same eyeline, this is beneath me, I don't recognise you. The other Nazis who had gone before him had the expression. I find it disturbing, this combination of blankness and arrogance where any other human might expect to see at minimum a trace of something else – remorse, horror, something human.

At that time the majority of the press corps thought he must be the last of them. He wasn't the biggest name despite that Eichmann smile – grimace. The court room had become a theatre of the perverse, the crowds diminishing as the 'Nazi personalities' did. Dead, convicted. But the law is the law. Dieter Geheimnis never denied he was an administrator at camp Z.

In the dock he exuded a kind of middle management pride – I was given a job, I executed it.

His appearance expressed contradiction – a jacket you might wear fishing in a Bavarian stream, a raffish scarf from Bohemia. At one point he rummaged through his jacket micro pockets.

A scrawled list was produced and unexamined presented to the judge.

From my position in the press area it was partially possible to decipher the list, a hieroglyph of names, numbers, images. The judge perused the document and looked up and back to the dock. The nod was almost imperceptible.

The conviction of Dieter Geheimnis felt like an ending, a drawing of a line. Some reporters expressed surprise at the length of the sentence, tempered by the type of jail most of it would be served in, a facility in suburban Berlin - hardly Spandau or Stammheim – where correction was expected to come not through punishment but gardening or water colouring. No doubt a tenured academic is preparing a PhD on Nazis and painting.

After work I occasionally flicked on ZDF or read a *Tagezeitung* feature by-lined Helena Gold, doyenne of Berlin's quality freelancers, about the ancient orderly of camp X or the accountant of camp Y but the definite articles were definitely trailing away. What was left to be said?

Gold wasn't the retiring type. The invitation to her retirement gathering was a surprise.

In the foyer of the Wintergarten Café she released me from an overdue hug. I had followed her by-lines deeper inside in the heavy press but it was sometime since we last met. Gold didn't forget crimes. I had moved from print to TV some time ago.

'Television,' she intoned, 'why did you do it?'

'Retirement,' I said, ' why are you doing it?'

'I was only following orders,' she said.

The laughter returned readily. Helena Gold had pursued so many gnarly Nazis to the courts and beyond at one point her editor said if you print the expression 'I was only following orders' again the investigative desk would be closed forever.

Three martinis later I asked her again: ' why did you do it, retire?'

'The epithet doyenne had become permanently inked to my name. Time to go .'

'But you hadn't finished,' I said

'I have, you haven't.' She passed a file to me. Everything in it was printed. Notes, cuttings, court circulars…'

'I haven't the attention span to read this,' I said, 'I'm in TV now. Executive summary.'

It was an almost smile. 'It's the future. Nazi hunting, guards, pond life. It's the past. This is where it's at. Art.'

'Art?'

'Do I have to say everything twice? You work in a visual medium. Forget tracking some 99-year-old functionary . Art is the big picture now. It's still out there. Read the file.'

'But…'

'It's an order,' she said. I looked up from the folder. She held my gaze for as long as she could. The lenses in her trademark spectacles were thickened each year to resemble the bottom of a Munich bier stein. 'I've been called to the bar.'

We fluffed the goodbye kiss - a scrawled note fell from the folder. She lit an unfiltered cigarette.

By the time the smoke cleared I was sitting on the terrace alone with the file.

I don't know how long it was before I felt someone standing behind me, the glow of a struck match illuminated the papers I was looking at in the dusk.

'What are you doing out here?' I said

Gold indicated the cigarette.

'Following orders.'

'Where did you get this?' I said, holding up a carbon copy of the note attached to a compliments slip of the state court.

'I never reveal my sources.'

She lit another cigarette from the remnants of the last one.

'I've given you enough.

I thought you'd be in Schillerpark by now. Missed the bus?'

I waited under the linden tree at the metro terminus. I reflected Schillerpark wasn't the most natural haunt of Nazis, ex or otherwise. I doubt if Dieter Geheimnis was aware of its proximity to Plötzensee, a centre of resistance. It was perhaps the suburb of Berlin that had least changed over the decades.

A lorry pulled up outside the apartment block. The driver kept the engine running.

The vehicle was adapted to carry glass or fragile panels on one side. There was a logo on the other side. I couldn't totally make it out.

I checked the address against one of the documents in the file. A punk emerged from doorway 33. Before it clicked shut I was in the stairwell. The lift was out of order.

The six flights of stairs gave me time to work out three questions. I tapped on the door. It was neither early or late, I was already inside the building, it never occurred to me he wouldn't open the door.

I heard him say 'One moment please.' There was a buzz and the door swung open from inside. I thought of the way the door of the open prison moved. Across the threshold I realised he was expecting someone else. I attributed my breathlessness to surprise not the stairs.

Herr Geheimnis was on the telephone. He spoke into the receiver:

'The lift is out of order. Come back tomorrow.'

This time he recognised me. He spoke again into the receiver - 'Please'- and turned to face me in one smooth movement, the black 40s style receiver uncradled.

'Good evening, Herr Schreiber. May I offer you some refreshment?'

Neutrality seemed to be the order of the evening. I wasn't going to complement his memory of the distant courtroom, his eyesight or his manners.

I accepted a Cognac. It was a remarkable vintage. I managed to compliment him on his taste. The drinks would give me more time, he wouldn't ask me to leave with a full glass.

'I have three questions, Herr Geheimnis, if I may.' The conversation was becoming like a scene from a von Stroheim film with dialogue.

'Ah, yes' he said, 'once a reporter always a reporter.'

'Firstly I never understood your sentence. The judge's summing up designated you a war criminal, the sentence was heavy though carried out in a place some of my colleagues in the popular press would describe as cushy. I obtained a carbon copy of the list you gave the judge. Why did you have it, why did you pass it to the judge, what has happened to all the items – or – people on the list?'

He indicated I should sit opposite him. He paused before answering. Peripherally I took in the room, classic 1944. There was only one painting on the walls, directly above him, his portrait, expressionist style. To his right, three steps leading possibly to an attic space. There was a lock on the door here like you see in a rented house where the landlord has locked away personal things off bounds to tenants.

He took in the movement of my eyes and stood next to the telephone table.

'It has been a most pleasant evening, Herr Schreiber. You have exceeded the number of your questions. You know the metro stop'

Outside the punk was on his way back. I held the door open for him. I switched my bag from off the shoulder to wrap around. 'Punks aren't Nazis,' he observed.

My own flat was at the opposite terminus. I poured a Cognac of my own. It tasted off compared to the brandy my host offered earlier in the evening.

Was there a pattern of incongruity, the expensive Cognac, the watch, the scarf, the antique telephone, the portrait? Things of quality, a bygone age, things that belonged to him but didn't seem to reflect him.

I awoke in my own armchair, the brandy bottle empty, the contents of the folder had slid to the carpet and were spread before me. I picked up the first item and dialled the number of the judge on the compliments slip. The judge himself answered rather than his office. My voice was harsh from the semi-sleepless night. I spoke without entirely processing my thoughts.

'Herr Vorsitzender Ritter? I apologise for calling you so early. My name is Schreiber.' I gave him the name of my old newspaper rather than my current TV station. 'I am closing the file on the Geheimnis case. There are some documents I wish to return to you. When would be convenient?'

The telephone at his end immediately clicked off. My coffee was filtering when my phone rang showing the last number I had dialled.

'Herr Schreiber? I would be honoured to see you.' He gave a private address in Charlottenburg.

The Judge showed me into his library. He stood opposite me. It was the only blank wall. Except for a portrait of the judge, similar style to the painting above Geheimnis.

'Thank you for seeing me,' I said, 'I apologise for the unearthly hour.'

'Is it,' he said 'unearthly?'

No refreshments were offered, it was a stand off. I could only fire off one question in the duel.

'Herr Vorsitzender, the Geheimnis case, he admitted to his war crimes but was assigned to what I would designate an open prison. An injunction enforced on journalists visits. He has most evidently not served a life sentence. Can you comment?'

'No'

He moved a step closer, I a step back. The diptych skilfully captured his disturbing eminent look: distinctive duelling scar on one side of his face, the burns from a Baader Meinhof car bomb on the other.

'A fascinating portrait, may I enquire about the painter?'

'No.'

'I apologise for troubling you at home.'

My hand was on the door handle. His right hand had remained in the pocket of his morning jacket throughout. It was only now outstretched. 'The documents you were returning, if you please, Herr Schreiber. It is an offence to make copies of documents from the prosecutor' s office.'

'I will return them to that office. Good day, Herr Vorsitzender.'

I immediately boarded the metro to my office. My mobile rang. I needed silence, staring out of the window as the department stores on the Ku'damm came to life.

My editor grinned knowingly. 'I see Helena Gold's bashes have not lost their epithet 'legendary'. If you are still nowhere on this Nazi looted art quest by close of play drop it. Nazis are history.'

I picked up the desk phone. 'State Prosecutor's Office. How may I direct your call?

'Herr Vorsitzender Ritter's office, please.'

'Herr Ritter?' There was a pause. 'Herr Ritter is no longer on the active bench list. I must redirect your call to the Federal Office for the Protection of the Constitution.'

I slammed the phone down.

The editor returned to my desk. 'Take the afternoon off. Go to an art gallery.' I picked up my mobile and began scrolling through my missed calls. 'You serious?' I said.

'Deadly,' she said. 'Fancy opening. Take full crew. Go home and put something decent on first. That's an order.'

I never use the adjective 'edgy.' The Mitte gallery wasn't my scene. The pictures on the wall didn't match my headache. But I was immediately glad I had chosen to go. The last period I was here was days celebrating the Wall fall. I was a non-date with Helena Gold. I noted she was more at ease in an art gallery than a newsroom. Each time she lit a cigarette you could make out the tattoo on her inner forearm. Numbers. She answered before I asked: 'I'll tell you about it once only, yeah? It is in honour of my mother. Camp R. If she had survived maybe one of her paintings would be here today.' The director of the art gallery joined us. Gold said ' Get us a drink. Darling'

The director was etched away not longer after – not that I am making a link – rumours of a plagiarised PhD never substantiated or dissipated.

The current director was continually referred to as new.

He came out to meet me and my crew in the foyer beneath the gallery logo, the design only been superficially made over.

'Have you got all the images you need?' he smiled. 'This evening is the official opening. The collection will be complete tomorrow.'

'What school would you call this?' I said. The style of the pictures was intriguing.

'Come into my office. We can do an interview if you want.'

'Is that what you want?' I said.

The crew set up the Klieg lights around his desk. Above him a portrait in the mode I recognised from my encounters with Geheimnis and Ritter.

The director saw my glance as a cue.

'You have commendable vision,' he said. He embarked on a dissertation unprompted-

'You will recall of course the history of the Nazis and the exhibition of so-called *Entartete Kunst?*

'I know my face looks lived in but I hardly remember 1937.'

The director brushed on-

'Most of the paintings and painters are now accounted for. But not all.

Provenance is the in word in my world. My predecessor Dr Hildegard took this most seriously. I regret she is not here to see the collection displayed this day. I'm sorry, this is of no interest to you…?'

My focus was fixed on the portrait. The intensity of the TV lights appeared to cause the surface paint to ripple and warp.

The director swivelled around in his Bauhaus replica. He stood facing the wall.

'Switch off the lights. Do it.'

He ran from his office into the main gallery. I gestured to the second cameraman to shoulder arms and follow. TV lights from other crews were illuminating a similar drama. All the abstracts were bubbling, sliding, beneath them bygone faces were appearing. Even the frames were melting. I stepped over the red cordon. Under the surface of the presented signature new signatures with numbers were visible. I had registered them before. They must be the names I had seen on the carbon copy of the list passed to Ritter from Geheimnis.

The director did not have the style to give orders. His efforts to make camera crews switch off lights were of no avail. Beneath each frame was now an oil slick, deathly faces on the portraits a living past.

I told my crews to keep filming and began my voiceover. This was live television.

I was in the moment. I never felt my mobile vibrate. My cameraman -producer said 'take this one, boss' He handed me his own phone.

'Yeah, what?' I said.

'I see you are Mr Big TV star but you need to get to Geheimnis. Now.

It was Helena Gold.

'I'm kind of in the middle of a story now', I said.

'Follow my orders for once, follow the story.'

'This must be your story too', I said, 'meet me outside his apartment block but don't, repeat, do not go in.'

'Alpha, charlie, tango, whisky or whatever' she forced a laugh.

I told my second cameraman to keep the live feed from the gallery going. Cameraman-producer Walter and I screeched off in the tech van.

We arrived at Schillerpark earlier than on my previous visit.

We waited.

'Anytime you want to make a move, boss?' said Walt.

'Get the equipment ready. We'll go on my command.'

'You stream too much TV'

The metro bus drew up behind us with a large sigh.

Helena Gold entered our VW.

'There isn't much time,' I said, ' feed me the questions.'

I looked at my watch.

An engine started up opposite us. I thought the bus was starting its return journey but it was the same lorry as the previous night, this time leaving with a load of frames attached to its side.

'Go, go, go,' I said to Walter. Gold gave me a look but followed, I didn't know she could move like that.

At door 33 the punk was setting out for his night.

'Thanks, man,' I said, taking the door from him.

We took the lift.

I pressed the buzzer marked Geheimnis.

'Herr Geheimnis. We have come directly from the Gallery. A most spectacular collection. We are sorry you could not be present at the display. The director would like you to do a television link.'

There was a pause.

A weak voice through the door: 'I always wanted to be on television, one day.'

The door opened silently.

Inside the figure of Dieter Geheimnis was virtually unrecognisable.

The almost miraculous sprightliness for a man his age was gone. The face was drawn, grey, shapeless, the smile ghastly.

I couldn't stand to look at him. Around the room was exactly as it was before, the single impassive portrait, the old telephone, the big radio, the *Volkischer Beobachter* stacked as matzos. There was no television.

I told Walt to stop filming.

I looked up the staircase to the attic. The latch lock was open. Inside only picture hooks.

'Speak, man,' Helena Gold urged me, 'before the answers go with him.'

'Is there anything you want to say? Who owns the pictures, what happened to the artists, why did you do what you did...'

He was on the floor, that nauseating grimace - smile all that remained.

'I ..I…was only following o...'

'Don't you dare,' Gold almost screamed at him. 'Stand up.'

'He's an old man,' I intervened.

'So?' said Gold.

'Lights on, I want this on the record,' she said to the cameraman-producer. Walt looked to me to second the order.

'You sit there,' she allowed Geheimnis that concession. She put a single chair beneath the portrait.

'Finally, exactly how did you obtain these paintings, why…?'

The stare from Geheimnis felt as hollow as the palimpsests we had witnessed in the gallery.

The glare from the Klieg lamps burned through the top surface of the picture. A picture developed, a woman, emaciated, terrified, dignified beautiful. There was no signature, only a row of numbers.

Gold put her forearm in front of the picture. The numbers matched.

Geheimnis moved his mouth, the words inaudible, what could he possibly say:

'I'm I'm s…'

Walter packed up the equipment before the ambulance arrived. Gold and I were on the metro to the Wintergarten. We sat on the terrace, three chairs, myself, Gold and the portrait. The waiter took in the triptych.

'You order,' said Helena Gold.

'Cognac,' I said. ' three of the finest.'

First serialized in *Second Generation Voices*
2022

SECOND GENERATION NETWORK

Also by **John F King** at **York Europe Publishing:**

Wise Guy and other fables, 2008

ISBN 978-0-955851902

> **Wise Guy,** 2012, is also available as an eBook at
>
> Smashwords ISBN 9781476351735

Drama King / 2010 ISBN

978-0-955851919

Funky / Guy and other micro-fiction, 2012 ISBN

978-0-955851964

Micro-Waves, 2012

ISBN 978-0-955851933

Vienna, Love, 2014

ISBN 978-0-955851971

Write Coach, 2014

ISBN 978-0-955851988

Write Coach II 2015

ISBN 978-0-9931306-1-8

A and E 2014

ISBN 978-0-955851995

Prog 2015

ISBN 978-0-9931306-0-1

What's Left 2016

ISBN 978-0-993106-2-5

Low – Rise 2016

ISBN 978-0-9931306-3-2

SW10 2017

ISBN 978-09931306-4-9

West End Story 2018

ISBN 978-0-993106-5-6

Nice People 2018

ISBN 978-0-99331306-6-3

Memories of the Future 2019 ISBN

978-09931306-7-0

4 x 4 2020

ISBN 978-0-9931306-8-7

Drama King II 2020

ISBN 978-1-716354335

Super-Over 2021

ISBN 978-1-8383426-0-9

Micro-Waves II

www.johnkinginternational.co.uk

JFKMedia

York Europe

ISBN 978-1-8383426-2-3

\

www.ingramcontent.com/pod-product-compliance
Lightning Source LLC
Chambersburg PA
CBHW080942170626
46811CB00009B/3223